This copy made possible by a generous
donation to the
Jackson County Library Foundation
from **Sherm and Wanda Olsrud.**

Jackson County Library
FOUNDATION

An Anteater Named
ARTHUR

by BERNARD WABER

ıpany · Boston

for Paulis

Library of Congress Catalog Card Number: 67-20374

Printed in the U. S. A.

ISBN: 0-395-20336-8 Reinforced Edition

ISBN: 0-395-25936-3 Sandpiper Edition

WOZ   40 39 38 37 36 35 34 33 32

Let me tell you about Arthur

First, I will tell you what Arthur is like
most of the time.
Most of the time, Arthur is a kind,
helpful,
understanding,
well-behaved,
sensible,
orderly,
responsible,
loving,
loveable,
altogether
wonderful
son.

BUT...

sometimes,
Arthur is a problem;
not all of the time, mind you,
just sometimes.
I will explain.

Sometimes Arthur doesn't understand

"I don't understand," says Arthur.

"What don't you understand?" I ask.

"We are called anteaters, right?"

"Right," I answer.

"Why must we be called by what we eat?"

"Because it happens that we are," I tell him.

"A cat eats fish, right?" Arthur asks.

"Right," I answer.

"A bird eats worms, right?"

"Right."

"A cow eats grass, right?"

"Right," I answer again.

"But the cat is not called a fisheater,
the bird is not called a wormeater,
and the cow is not called a grasseater.
Right?" Arthur asks.
"Right," I answer.

"Then I shall be called by another name."

"What will you be called?" I ask.

"I shall be called a 'blion.'"

"But you are not a 'blion,'" I tell him.

"Then I shall be called a 'swhale.'"

"But you are not a 'swhale.'"

"Then I shall be called a 'melephant.'"

"But you are not a 'melephant.'"

"Then I shall be called a 'brabbit.'"

"But you are not a 'brabbit.'"

"What shall I be called?" Arthur asks.

"You shall be called an anteater," I tell him.
"An anteater named Arthur."

Sometimes Arthur has nothing to do

"I have nothing to do," says Arthur.

"Why don't you call on a friend?" I suggest.

"Who?" Arthur asks.

"How about William?"

"William is not my friend."

"How about Thomas?"

"Thomas is not feeling well."

"How about Patrick?"

"Patrick is being punished."

"How about Bertram?"

"Bertram is having company."

"How about Maria?"

"Who?"

"Maria."

"Maria is a girl."

"So?"

"So I don't play with girls."

"Maria can throw a ball," I mention.

"She throws like a girl."

"Why don't you read a book?"

"I have read all of my books."

"How about playing records?"

"The record player is broken."

"You can work with your microscope."

"I did that this morning."

"Well," I say, "I have one more suggestion.
Since you have nothing to do, and I have much
to do, you can spend the day helping me."
"Doing what?" Arthur asks.
"Well, there are things to be carried up
to the attic. The shelves in the pantry need
straightening. The garden could be weeded.
And . . ."

Arthur puts on his hat and jacket.
"Where are you going?" I ask.

"I think I will go and see what
Maria is doing," he answers.

Sometimes Arthur's room
is more than I can believe

"Arthur!" I exclaim.
"Your room is more than I
can believe."
Arthur looks about his room.
"I don't see anything,"
he answers.

"You don't see anything!" I reply.
"You don't see that your cover is on the
floor, your pillow is on the bureau,
your pajamas are under the bed, your best tie
is hanging from the light fixture and there
are bits of paper scattered everywhere?"

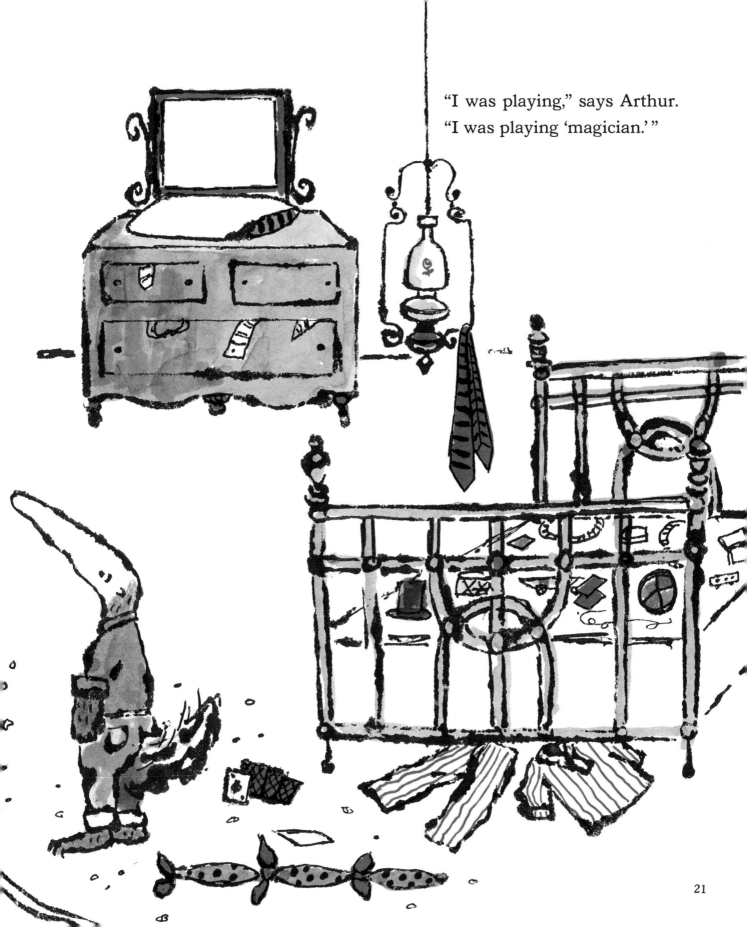

"I was playing," says Arthur.
"I was playing 'magician.'"

"Are you a magician?" I ask.

"Yes," Arthur answers.

"Are you a very good magician?"

"Yes, I am a very good magician."

"Can you make things appear and disappear?"

"Yes, I can make things appear and disappear."

"Very well," I say, "how would you like to
perform a magic trick for your mother?"

"I would like it," Arthur answers.

"What kind of trick?"

I explain the trick:

"I will leave the room. I will close
the door. Later, when I open it again,
I will want to see if, by magic, you have
made some things appear where they
should appear, and some things disappear
that should disappear. All right?"

"All right," Arthur answers.

"Ready?"

"Ready," says Arthur.

"Get set!"

"Set," says Arthur.

"Go!"

I close Arthur's door.

Later, I open his door.
"Look!" says Arthur. "The magic
trick has worked."

"You are a good little magician," I tell him.
"And that was a very good trick."

Sometimes Arthur is choosy.

"Breakfast! Breakfast is ready!"
I call to Arthur.

Arthur comes down.
"What are we having?" he asks.
"We are having ants," I answer.

"What kind of ants?"
"The red ones," I tell him.
Arthur makes a face.
I pretend not to notice.

"Look at them," I say in my cheeriest voice,
"aren't these the most beautiful ants
you have ever seen . . . in all your life?
I gathered them especially for you."
Arthur looks and makes another face.
"Arthur," I go on, "red ants are delicious;
and so good for you too. Don't you want
to grow up to be big and strong; as big and as
strong as your father? Have you watched
your father eat red ants?"
More faces from Arthur.

"I have an idea," I say,
"how about if I sprinkle
sugar on them?
Red ants are simply
delightful with sugar."
Arthur shakes his head.
"A twist of lemon, perhaps?"
More head shaking from Arthur.

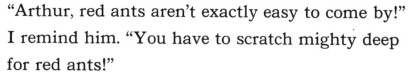

"Arthur, red ants aren't exactly easy to come by!"
I remind him. "You have to scratch mighty deep
for red ants!"
Arthur begins playing with his spoon.

"You ought to at least try one," I continue.
"You will never know if you like something unless
you give it a chance. Here, how about this one?"
"Ilk!" says Arthur,
turning his head away.

"Very well!" I exclaim at last, "never mind about the red ants. Never mind that you are missing out on the world's tastiest, most delicious, most scrumptuous dish. What will you eat instead?"

"Brown ants," Arthur answers.

Sometimes Arthur forgets

"Goodbye," says Arthur,
rushing off to school.
"Goodbye," I say.
The door closes.

The door opens.

"What did you forget?" I ask.

"I forgot my spelling book,"
he answers.

Up he runs,
two steps at a time.

Down he comes with
his spelling book.

"Goodbye," says Arthur.
"Goodbye," I say.
The door closes.

39

The door opens.
"What did you forget?" I ask.
"I forgot my sneakers,"
he answers.

Up he runs,
two steps at a time.

Down he comes with
his sneakers.

"Goodbye," says Arthur.
"Goodbye," I say.
The door closes.

41

The door opens.

"What did you forget?" I ask.

"I forgot my pencil case," he answers.

Up he runs,
two steps at a time.

Down he comes with
his pencil case.

"Arthur," I say to him, "you will have to
try to remember not to forget. Now stop and
think. Do you have everything you need?"
"Yes," Arthur answers.
"You are absolutely, positively, without a
shade of a doubt, one hundred percent sure now?"
"Yes, I am absolutely, positively, without a
shade of a doubt, one hundred percent sure," he answers.

"Goodbye then."

"Goodbye," says Arthur.

The door closes.

I wait to see if it will open again.

I am not disappointed.
The door opens.
"What did you forget?" I ask.
"I forgot to kiss you goodbye,"
he answers.

"Goodbye," says Arthur.

"Goodbye," I say.

The door closes.

See what I mean about Arthur.